SECRETS OF A SUGAR BABY 4

SUGAR BABY SECRETS BOOK 4

MIA BLACK

Blake

"Jae? What's wrong? Why are you looking like that?"

Just then, I heard a voice travel from behind me. Her eyes widened and, in a moment's notice, she seemed to float right by me. Confused, I spun around to see who it was behind me that she was headed to. He stood tall with his arms out and a cocky smile on his face as if he knew she wouldn't resist him. *Non-sense.* "Um, Jae? Jae, where are you going?"

She all but ignored me as she headed for the man who stood just down the pathway. I could feel the anger bubbling in my veins. My hands balled into fists. I knew I couldn't take him in a fight. He was much too big for me to handle on my own, but if he thought he was going to come between me and Jae, he had another thing coming.

"Jae!" I said louder and with more impatience, but she didn't respond. She wrapped her arms around him as he lifted her off her feet and twirled her around as if I wasn't even there. My eyebrows furrowed as I watched the two of them in front of me.

Just then, I looked just beyond them to my vehicle. I signaled to my henchmen for them to get out of the car and handle whoever this was in front of me. I didn't have time for the disrespect and whatever was going on between them was going to stop now. They approached him and snatched Jae out of his grasp.

"Aye, man, what the fuck?! You betta' let go of me! Who the fuck are you?!"

Jae screamed out, "What are you doing?! I know him! Let him go! Get off of me!"

She tried to fight my men off as they carried her back to me while the tall man struggled to break free from my henchmen. When she came back to me, I glared at her in the eyes. "Do you think I am going to let you go to another man like that? I told you once, and I'll tell you again. You are mine and I am not having you with anyone else, so you may as well get that out of your head right now. Do you understand me?"

My henchmen punched her wannabe lover in the stomach and sent him crumbling to his knees. I had to teach him a lesson. If he didn't understand it now, he wouldn't understand it later. He had to know that Jae would be off limits to him. Not just now, but for as long as I wanted. She was mine.

I SNAPPED out of the daydream as Jae continued with her arms wrapped around him. I didn't understand what was going on, but I needed answers. I needed answers before I allowed my anger to get the best of me.

CHAPTER 1

Jae

I couldn't believe that he was standing in front of me, let alone with his arms wrapped around me. I didn't think I would see him again any time soon, especially after everything I'd done in the past few weeks. If it wasn't for Blake clearing his throat behind me, I would've forgotten that he was even there. I let Darryl go and cleared my throat. "I'm sorry. Um, Blake? This is my friend, Darryl. I've known him since we were children. We grew up together."

"Umhmm," he said, eying Darryl.

"Darryl, this is um, this is Blake. A good friend of mine."

The two of them exchanged glares at each other. I knew that they both had animosity building up between them, but I didn't want it to bubble into anything that I couldn't control, so I spoke up again. "So, Blake, thank you for everything. I am glad that we got Shayla out of the way and I hope that she does all the time that they can give her."

"Yes, I as well," he said as his eyes continued on Darryl. I reached in to give him a hug. He wrapped his arms around me, then kissed me on the forehead. "Will I see you later?"

"Um, just give me a call. I don't think I will be busy."

"Alright."

We released each other and as he walked toward the vehicle, he didn't acknowledge Darryl. Darryl shrugged his shoulders and once Blake got into his car, he stepped forward. "So, is that the dude that you have been messing with?"

I exhaled and shook my head. I didn't want to say anything to ruin the moment. He had just gotten here and I knew that he would leave just as fast if I said something he didn't like. I grabbed his hand. "Come in; I know somebody else in here can't wait to see you."

I unlocked the door and pulled him inside. "Angie? Angie, where are you at? Guess who I found outside our door."

Moments later, she walked into the living room. She smiled ear to ear when she saw Darryl standing in the doorway. "Oh, my God! Darryl!" She sprinted and ran into his arms as the two of them embraced. I enjoyed their relationship. It was truly a brother and sister vibe that they had with each other and if it wasn't for her, I don't think we would have remained as close. She was the glue between me and Darryl and I appreciated her for that.

"Yeah," he said as they released each other, "I figured that I would just pop up and surprise yall, you know? Return the favor since Jae did it to me a little while ago."

"Well, shoot," she said as she grabbed his hand and pulled him to the couch, "I am glad you did! I was just talking to Jae about you the other day. Come on, sit down! Sit!" We all sat down on the couches in the living room. I sat on one end, Darryl in the middle and Angie on the other side of him. "So," she continued, "I know you will be happy to hear that I stopped strippin'."

"Word? You did?"

"Yes. I quit that bullshit and started the LPN program. I enrolled a little while back and I just started classes last week!"

"For real? That's wassup, Angie! I knew you could do better than what you were doing. It would just take some time."

"Hell yeah, and I'm glad as fuck that I got away from that shit. It feels like I have a real life now, you know? Like, I an't gotta worry about niggas feelin' on me and tryin' to pay me extra just to let them stick they tiny little dicks inside of me. I respect myself too much to keep puttin' up with that shit, so I left and started a better life for myself."

"Yeah, no doubt. Shit, well, if it is anything I can do to help you out in that, just let me know. You know I got you."

"Yeah."

I looked at Angie. I knew she was happy to see Darryl, but I wanted some time alone with him. I just didn't know how to say it without being rude. She picked up on the clue. "And, you know what? Come to think of it, I need to study for a test I got coming up next week. So—" She stood up. "I'ma leave yall two alone so yall can catch up. I know yall probably got a lot to talk about."

She smiled and with that, she left the two of us alone in the front room. "That girl really loves you," I said as I looked at Darryl.

"Yeah, the feeling is mutual. That is my sis and I would go to war for her. No doubt about it. But, she is not the only reason I came through."

He smiled at me. I blushed and quickly turned my head away from him. I couldn't stand the enchanting glow of his smile. It was too much for me to bear right now. I stood up and extended my hand. Without saying a word, he got up, connected with mine and then I led him into my room and closed the door behind us.

He plopped down on the bed. "Um, you really about to put your size 12's on my covers like that?"

He laughed. "Shit, my bad. You know that's how I used to do back in the day."

"Yeah, and I snapped on yo' ass back then when you did it, too. I don't know what little hoes you messin' with that let you put yo' shoes all over their shit, but I ain't the one." He kicked off his shoes. They made a thud when they hit the ground.

"Is that better?"

"Much better," I said as I sat down on the bed next to him. I knew we had a lot to talk about. He had questions and I hoped that he woudn't be more upset once I gave him the answers. I exhaled. "So, I'ma just come out and tell you. I mean, I don't have to tell you because I now you already know or have heard about it. But, the sex tape. Listen, I'm sorry. It is me on there and I don't know what I was thinking to let myself get involved with something like that. I was so stupid and silly and I should've just left it all alone. You felt like I was a whore and honestly, I was. I mean, I felt like one. Hell, who am I kidding, I was one. I just—"

"Yo', I'm not gon' let you do that to yourself, Jae."

"Huh?"

"I'm not gon' let you belittle yourself like that." He scooted closer to me and put his hand on my thigh. "Look, it was wrong of me to judge you and your situation. I don't know what you were going through and what you needed at the time. All I did was come at you and expect you to be this perfect version that I wanted. I didn't look at it from your point of view and it was selfish of me. You are not a hoe. You are nothing like that. You just did what you had to do and I'm not holding it against you."

Tears started to form in my eyes. That was the last thing I expected to hear from him, but it was one of the reasons why I loved him so much. He always said the right things, no matter what time it was. "I was just angry, Jae. That's why I said all of that shit and walked out on you. That's why I wasn't returning your calls or anything. Yeah, you slept with another nigga, but I've slept with bitches, too. I had to stop bein' like that because there ain't a female in the world that hasn't slept with at least one nigga before they ended up marrying somebody else. It was immature to think that way, but you know, in my mind, that's how it was. So, I apologize."

He took my hand and kissed the back of it, then slowly moved up my arm. I loved him even more after he said all of that. To think that I was just going to let him walk away and never reach out to him again? That was enough to break me down into more tears. He pulled me close to him and we both laid down in my bed.

He kissed me on the back of the neck and pulled me close. "Yo', remember when we used to just hold each other back in the projects? You would be scared to stay there alone while you waited for Angie to come back, so I just held you all night? We didn't fuck or nothing. That's when I knew I loved you for real. If a nigga can lay with you and not try to fuck? Consistently? Shit, that is the difference between lust and love. That's how I knew the difference."

CHAPTER 2

"So, that was that nigga, huh? The one that I ran into outside. He was the one in the tape that was floating around on social media and shit?"

I huffed. I didn't want to talk about it, but he had a right to know as much as he wanted to. "Yes, that was him. I regretted what I was doing, but I had to do it. It was the position I was in. Like, I needed to make money and I didn't want to strip. So, I ran into this company. Sugar baby. They weren't escorts or anything like that. We would just get paid to spend time with men. Sometimes, it led to sex, but sometimes, it was just spending time with another person. Old men with money get lonely just like anybody else. They would rather pay someone to spend time with them than to find someone who wanted to kill them because of their money. They were always so paranoid. That is a life I would never want to live because it sounds like hell to me. But, anyways, that is what I did."

"Damn. So, you were just paid to date people? Shit, that doesn't sound bad at all if you never had to have sex with them."

"I didn't have to, Darryl. Sometimes, it just happened. The same way it did with Blake."

He stroked my arm with his hand as the moonlight shined through the bedroom window. I thought back to the time we spent cuddled together in my twin bed back in my room in the projects. The nights we spent talking to each other through the night. It was peaceful. Something that I missed. Something that I yearned for. "So, do you love him?"

"What?"

He laughed. "You heard me. Stop stalling. I said do you love him?"

"No, Darryl. Well, not like that. I mean, I care about him. I love him as a friend, you know? We built a good relationship over time and all, but I am not in love with him. There is a difference. You know that, right?"

He exhaled. "Yeah, I know the difference between the two. I just want to be sure that you are being real with yourself. I mean, if you love the nigga, just let me know. It won't take much to kill that nigga so we don't have to worry about him."

I elbowed him in the stomach. "Boy, shut up talkin' stupid. You ain't about to murder nobody and fuck up your life like that. You are a star basketball player and, on top of that, I know you are headed for the league. Stop talkin' stupid."

"Nah, you don't know if I am headed to the league. As good as I am, that shit is out of my control. All it takes is one injury or one person not to like you. After that, the rumors start and draft stock drops. It is all a crap shoot, you feel me? A gamble. But with you? I don't want to gamble. I want everybody to know that they don't have a chance with you and if I gotta off a nigga for it, then so be it."

I popped him again. "Boy, stop it! Stop talkin' like that because you are going to piss me off. I told you that I am not in love with him, so none of that even matters. Stop talkin' stupid." He kissed me on the top of the head and I snuggled back into his arms. "But, now that I quit all of that, I can't front. I am scared. I don't know what to expect. I don't know what is out there."

"What do you want to do?"

"Go back to school. I want to get involved in fashion, you know? Run a business. Run my own clothing store. Something like that. That is what is in my heart to do."

"Ok. So, do it. There shouldn't be anything stopping you right now."

"Easier said than done."

"How is that?"

"Because it costs money, Darryl. A lot of money that I don't have right now. I mean, I have money saved up from working at sugar baby, but other than that, there ain't nothing there to spend. Not for school, at least. I need a job to be able to pay tuition, but because of that punk ass sex tape that got leaked, nobody wants to hire me. They are afraid of the attention that it will bring."

"Damn. I can see that being the reason why. Shit. Yeah, that tape—that tape was some shit. But yo', what if I said I could help you."

"Help me? Help me how?"

"You know I got my scholarship and I don't want to brag, but it ain't nothin for me to pull some strings on campus and find a way to get you a few of them as well. I'm tellin' you, them folks up at that school will bend over backwards to make me happy. Shit, with all the money I am bringing into that school, they better be lucky that I don't ask for much at all. They owe me."

"I don't know, Darryl. I don't want you abusing your power just to get me on at your school. I can do it myself."

"How?"

"I can figure it out."

"Bullshit. If you could figure it out, then you would have by now. Look, what you need to do is just sit yo' ass back and let yo' man take care of this shit. Something you should've did from the jump. Then maybe you wouldn't be involved in this bullshit you are in right now."

"My man? Excuse me, but when the fuck did you become my man?"

"Just now. You got a problem with it?"

I looked over my shoulder at him as he waited for a response. After a few seconds of silence went by, I snuggled back into his arms. "You are lucky I am in love with you. Otherwise, I wouldn't let you talk to me like that."

"Umhm. Anyways, you need to get used to it though. I got you. Just let me handle this shit."

"How long are you going to be in town?"

"I am on spring break, so I'll be here for a week."

"A week? Ok. It is short, but I'll take it."

CHAPTER 3

The next morning, I woke up before Darryl. I watched him lay asleep beneath the covers next to me. It was comforting to lay with a man and not have him expect to have sex that same night. It was something that I admired about him. Something on top of the things that I already loved. I kissed him on the cheek, then got up so I could go and make breakfast for us.

I checked in Angie's room as I walked down the hallway. Her bed was made and the room was spotless. I figured she was in the kitchen already, but when I went in, the room was already cleared. I sent her a text message to see where she was at. "Hey, I'm at school. I had class this morning."

"Oh, ok. I was about to make breakfast, so I just wanted to be sure. I'm proud of you, sis. Keep going!"

I smiled and put the phone down, then went to the kitchen to prepare breakfast for me and Darryl. I imagined us together later in life, doing much of the same thing. Him upstairs in the bed, tired from basketball practice while I was in the kitchen, cooking and keeping the house clean. I didn't expect to be a stay-at-home mom and it was not what I wanted, but I knew that Darryl would make it hard for me to do anything else. Not because he was controlling, but because I knew he wouldn't want me to work if I didn't have to. I grabbed the eggs, bacon and mixed pancake batter, then started cooking our meal.

"It smells good in here, baby," he said as he stepped into the kitchen, shirtless. I was just about done cooking as he wrapped his arms around me from behind, then leaned down to kiss me on my neck. "And you look good. I see I got the best of both worlds this morning."

"Thank you. I figured I would show a little bit of hospitality while you were here. Didn't want to send you off thinking that I treated you like a second-class citizen."

He laughed. "Nah, I wouldn't have thought that. The only thing you had to do was show me some attention. Anything else is extra." He kissed me again, then took his plate off the stove. "But I will definitely take the extra."

"How do you know that plate is yours?"

He took a slice of bacon off and crunched it into his mouth. "Because it was the one I picked. You know you don't eat that much anyway, so don't try to act like the plate without a lot of food on it was supposed to be mine."

I rolled my eyes, grabbed the other plate off the stove and sat down with him at the table. I loved how he knew me like the back of his hand. We were meant to be, I just didn't believe that we would ever get together. "So, last night. What you were saying about being my man. Were you serious about that?"

He nodded his head. "Yeah, dead serious. What? You think I'ma let that nigga Blake step in the picture and try to take you away from me? Nah. It ain't goin' down like that. I'm letting him, and everybody else know right out the gate that you are with me."

"I told you that Blake is not anyone to worry about. I am not in love with him, but, he did help me along the way. He gave me a lot of motivation to get somewhere else in life. I appreciate him from that standpoint, but other than that, that's all it is."

He crunched down on another strip of bacon. "That's all, huh? So, in what ways did he motivate you?"

"Well, college for one. He made it seem like a possibility for me. Like, I guess I was just in the mindset of working at sugar baby and I didn't see any other way, but he put that bug in my ear and after that, I kind of ran with it. I mean, before, it was just a thought but now? Now, it seems like something that can actually happen."

"Hell yeah, it can, Jae. I mean, you are smart as shit. One of the smartest women I've known. I know you can go to college and get shit done. As a matter of fact, since I'm out for a week, you should let me take you on some college tours, you know? See if you find one that you like or, at the least, get a better idea of how things will be whenever you enroll."

"Really? No, I can't ask you to do that. Go back to school on your break away from school? That is so unfair."

He laughed, then took a knife and sliced one of his pancakes. "If you think I actually do work when I am at school, you got me fucked up. I don't do anything but hoop and kick it most of the time. Other times, I got people feeding me test scores and shit just so I can keep my scholarship.”

“Darryl!”

He laughed again. “You know I am just fuckin’ around with you. I am serious about my education, especially since I know this NBA shit is not guaranteed. But, either way, I don’t mind showing you around some other campuses just so you can get an idea of how shit will be. I think it will be good for you.”

I thought about what he said. The more he floated the idea around in my head, the more I was anxious about checking things out for myself. I knew I was headed in the right direction, I just wasn’t sure if I wanted to take all that time just to study and get a degree. I needed money, and a career, a lot sooner than the four or five years it would take to graduate.

“Alright, let’s do it. I’m going to go and get my laptop so I can start looking at some school around here that I want to visit.”

“Aight, cool.”

I winked at him, then took my last piece of bacon with me back to my room so I could research a few schools. When I got to the room, I picked up his shirt off the floor and folded it, then put it in the chair next to the dresser. I slid his Jordans to the side just underneath the bed, then crawled onto the mattress with my laptop and started looking for schools in the area.

In the end, I thought it would be good to go to Darryl's school with him, but I didn't want to make it seem like I was smothering him. I was sure that he had his women on campus and I didn't want to get involved in any drama while I was trying to get my education. Finally, he came into the room with me and flopped down onto the bed.

"Ugh. You see I am trying to do some work. You got the laptop moving all around on the mattress because you want to jump on the bed like a little kid."

"Yeah, yeah, yeah," he said as he slapped my hand. My thumb hit the mouse on the keyboard. "Wait a minute. What is that?"

He pointed to a heart folder on my desktop. "It is a heart."

"Shit, I know that, but I'm sayin'. What is in it?"

That folder had been there for so long that I forgot it was on the home screen. I didn't want him to see it yet, but it was too late since he already laid eyes on it. "Shoot! You weren't supposed to see it!"

"See what? That heart? What? Is it pictures of you and that fake ass playboy nigga Blake in there? Is that why you didn't want me to see it?"

"Uh, no. Not at all."

"Then what is it, Jae? Open the folder so I can see who you got inside that little heart shaped shit. Unless you think it is gon' piss me off. And, if it's gon' make me mad, then just forget it. I don't need to see it. As a matter of fact—"

I sucked my teeth. "Hold on before you get all in yo' chest and start an argument that is not even necessary." I double clicked the folder. "Here, you little cry baby."

He took the laptop away from me. I scooted closer to him as his eyes widened in front of me. He clicked picture after picture, him and his grandmother filled the folder. "Damn," he said as he looked at me, "damn. How did you get all of these pictures? Look at me. Damn, I was so little. With a big ass head, too!"

"Well, some shit never changes."

He smirked. "Ha, ha, ha. Nah, but for real, how did you get all of these pictures?"

"Well, after your grandma died, I went into her place and searched it with you. I found a shoebox with a bunch of pictures inside of it. So, I grabbed them and tucked them away. I was going to put it all together in a collage as a gift for you when you graduated from college. But, now I guess you have just ruined that, huh?"

He barely paid any attention to me as he scrolled through the pictures. "Wow," he said, smiling, "look at my grandma. She was so fucking pretty. You would've never guessed that she had a mouth on her though, would you?"

"Nope, not at all. I still can't believe she used to cuss you out. I can't imagine her doing that."

"Yeah, that was before she got saved. She used to be wild. Well, not real wild, but just wild with the way she spoke." He exhaled and shook his head, then looked towards me. "You said this was going to be a gift for me after I graduated from school?"

"Yup. I had it planned out and everything. I was going to throw you a party and then have a projector screen up so everyone could see you and your big head ass when you were a baby. They would see how you progressed from that and into the fine, college educated man that we all see today. I thought it would be special for you."

"You thought it would be? Man, there is no question that it would've been special. Shit, it still is special, for real."

I could tell he was fighting tears when he spoke to me. I scooted closer to him, "well, you are special to me, Darryl. Very special. More than you know. I just want you to understand that and I wanted to give you something to show that I've been there with you from the beginning and I hope to be there with you until the end."

After he clicked the last picture, he picked the laptop up and put it to the side, then wrapped his arms around me. "Man, that is all I want. I want you to be here with me to the end and honestly, I don't see it any other way. I haven't and I never will."

He leaned in to kiss me on the lips. I grinded on top of him. He put his hands on the bottom of my shirt and lifted it over my head, exposing my round breasts and erect nipples. He licked his tongue around their firmness as I squirmed, the sensation sent chills through over body before he engulfed my breasts inside of his mouth.

I reached my hands into his shorts until I wrestled his penis free from its cage and without warning, I removed myself from his lap and slid my mouth around it. Darryl leaned his head back as I licked the shaft of his penis and messaged his balls with the other hand. "Yes," he moaned in a voice that was barely audible as slid his dick completely inside my mouth. The tip of it brushed against the back of my throat until I pulled the saliva covered penis out of my mouth.

I licked the shaft and wrapped my hand around his dick as he stood up and grabbed me by the waist. He flipped me upside down with ease and planted his mouth right onto my vagina as I slid my mouth back around his dick. I dug my nails into his buttocks as he brushed his tongue over my clit and sent a thunderous vibration through my legs until a rush of moisture exploded from my pussy.

He let me down and tossed me onto the bed, but like a magnet, his dick was drawn right to my vagina as he mounted me and pinned my legs back by my head. My titties bounced up and down as he pounded me, his muscular chest bulging with each time he moved slowly inside of me. "Yes, baby. Yes," I moaned, pushing him deeper inside. He pushed his lips against mine and twirled his tongue around in my mouth as I gripped onto the edge of the mattress. "Again," I said in a breath devoid of life, "I'm coming again."

I missed this feeling. I never had it when I had sex with Blake or anyone else. It was what separated true love from the lust that was going on between me and another man. With Darryl, I knew what it was. He loved me and I wanted this to last forever. I pulled away from him, glaring into his eyes. My reflection bounced off his irises. The passion filled the room like steam out of a shower. He stroked my hair. "I love you," he said as he dead-locked with my eyes.

"I love you too, baby. Don't hurt me."

"I will never hurt you."

A tear rolled down the side of my face as he slowly moved inside of me. I locked my legs around him and with each slow thrust, I could feel him expressing how deep his love for me and how deep my love for him went. He touched every inch of my depth. His dick stroked every spot that belonged to him. Every place in my body and in my heart that hadn't been reached by anyone. It was his and, for as long as I could remember, it had always been his.

I pressed my nails into his back like a baby koala as I peaked, my legs shook vigorously each time he moved in and out of me. Moments later, I felt his cum shoot inside of me, and as his penis jumped, I licked my lips and sucked my finger like it was his dick. "Wait a minute," he said as he moved down to my vagina. "I want to taste it."

He stuck his tongue into my vagina as I put my hands on the back of his head, gliding him around as he twirled his tongue inside of me like a ballerina. Suddenly, he lifted my legs onto his shoulders and balanced me as he stood up and pinned me against the wall. He licked my pussy while I was pinned against the wall. The thrill increased the intensity of my ecstasy. We flipped back and forth between making love and fucking all morning. I pinned my hands against his head as he French kissed my lips and danced his tongue around my clitoris until I felt my legs shaking on his shoulders.

I looked down at him as he moved his head back and forth. "Yes," I said in a voice that was barely audible. Minutes later, I came again. His tongue slurped every bit of moisture from my pussy and into his mouth as I moaned out loud, my legs squeezing around his neck like a boa constrictor. He walked over to the bed and laid me down as I panted on her back. From behind, he climbed on top of me like a lion pouncing on its prey.

He took one leg and held it up as he thrusted himself into me without remorse. My mouth hung open as if I wanted to scream but couldn't get the sound to leave my throat. He pounded me from behind as he grabbed a handful of my hair and yanked it towards him. I pounded on the mattress as pain mixed perfectly with pleasure. He smacked my ass with so much force that I felt the sting for minutes after he hit it. He pushed himself deeper inside of me as he came again and with that, I yelled out loud.

He shoved my head into a pillow to muffle my screams. His dick was bigger than I remembered as he bent me over from behind and spread my cheeks as far as they would go. I smacked the mattress with an open hand as he held my waist steady and thrusted himself deeper inside of me. I felt his dick jump, and at that moment, I knew he was coming again. Soon after, he plopped down onto the mattress beside me, breathing heavy like he had just run a mile.

"I could definitely get used to this," I said, facing the ceiling with the covers halfway over my body.

"Yeah, so could I."

CHAPTER 4

"You ready now?"

"Boy, don't you even start with me."

"I've been out here on this couch for the last two hours waiting for you to come out here. Who you trying to get dressed for? With them jeans and the heels. We just going to look at some colleges, you not goin' on a job interview."

"Well." I stood sideways in the long mirror to look at my shape as I ran my hand over my curves. "You know what they say about first impressions. I don't need them thinking that I am just some run of the mill chick. They need to know that I am serious."

He stood up and pulled me closer to him. I felt his hard abs against my back. "Well, we are about to be late because I'm getting ready to rip them clothes off you and start round, what? Four?"

I laughed and pushed away from him, "Darryl, no! We can't. You made these appointments and we can't be late. I don't want to look bad in front of them or give a bad impression. Come on, we have more than enough time to pick up on round four, five or twenty-five later. Ok?"

He winked at me, then slapped me on the behind. "Aight. That sounds good to me. But, let's get goin'. We got a full day ahead of us."

"Ok, daddy. I'm ready."

He leaned forward, kissed me on the cheek, and after that, we made our way to the first college. He parked in the lot just ahead of the administrative building. As soon as I got out of the car, I was taken back by everything. The school spirit planted on every light post in the parking lot. The students walking with school gear representing the university, all with smiles on their faces. It was something that I wanted to be a part of as soon as I saw it.

He met me on my side of the car and extended his hand.

"You ready to go in?" he asked, breaking me out of my daydream.

"Yes. Yes, I am ready."

I smiled and with that, we made our way into the building. The spacious hallways almost felt too large. School posters hung from the walls as we walked down the corridor. A few people smiled our way. The women looked at Darryl, but once they saw me next to him, they quickly shifted their attention. "Boy, if you turn your head to look at those girls' booties, we are going to fight."

He laughed. "Shit, I know better than that. You look for me and tell me what they look like."

I rolled my eyes, then turned my head to catch a glance. "Yeah, they are thick. Well, the one on the left is. The one on the right is ok." When I faced forward, I caught Darryl just turning his head back to the front. I elbowed him in the side with a smile. "Boy, I told you not to look! Is that how it is?"

He pulled me close as we walked down the hallway. "Baby, I got the queen bee right here, bzzzzz. You are the only one that I'ma ever put my stinger in."

"Yeah, yeah, I can tell why you are a basketball player

instead of a writer. If I am the bee, then how are you going to have the stinger?"

He sucked his teeth. "Why you tryin' to be technical? Just appreciate the fact that I only want to look at other girls, but I want to love, fuck and be with you. That's my word, Jae. I love you."

I smiled and took hold of his hand again. "I love you too, baby."

He winked at me and then led me down the hallway and into the administrative office. "Hello," one of the ladies behind the desk said as we came into the room. "How can we help you two today?"

"I have a meeting with Bryan Taylor of admissions."

"Oh, right. Ok. I will page Mr. Taylor. Go ahead and have a seat and he will be with you in a moment."

"Thank you."

We sat down in the office. Students walked past the room, laughing and talking loudly with each other. It reminded me of high school and from what I could tell, college was just a bigger version of that with a lot less restrictions. It was a part of my life that I had skipped over as soon as I started working for sugar baby. I thought that life would be the best route for me because, at the time, I felt like school was a waste of time. A way for people to get hustled and spend money to get degrees that they would never use. To an extent, I still believed that, but for me, the experience was what I wanted. The fact that I could add another accomplishment to my title. I wanted that and I was sure that, in some way, it would open up doors for me in the future. I just wasn't sure how.

Minutes later, Mr. Taylor stepped into the office, smiling from ear to ear. He extended his hand to Darryl first as he stood to his feet. "Darryl?" he asked.

"Yes, sir."

"I am Mr. Taylor. My, you are tall."

"Yes, I am putting my height to good use, too."

"I hope you'll be playing ball for us."

He smiled. "No, sir. I am already enrolled. I play at the university."

He snapped his fingers. "You know what? I recognize you now. You are projected to go in the lottery whenever you commit to the draft."

"Yeah, that is what I hear. But—" He looked at me. "I am

here to get some information for my future wife. She wants to get back into school, so I am taking her on tours of a few different schools in the area so she can get an idea of what things would be like."

"Well," he looked at me, "I am glad that you two have stopped here. Hopefully during this visit, I can persuade you to come along here. Well, if you two will follow me, we are going to stop in my office for a quick second so I can grab a few things, and then we will start the tour."

"Sounds good."

He walked ahead of us as I looked at Darryl. "You two were really starting a bromance a few minutes ago. I was just going to walk out and leave the two of you alone so yall could get to know each other better."

"Ha. Yeah, real funny. If anything, that might have just helped you get in. If they know I am going to the league, they might bend over backwards to get you in with the hopes that I will 'remember that' once you are enrolled. Colleges are always looking for donations from big time athletes. I might be your golden ticket in more ways than one."

"Whatever. I don't need your golden ticket, thank you. I can do this on my own."

"My bad, baby girl," he said with a smile. "You got it."

Mr. Taylor led us through the hallways of the first building. I was taken back by how big it was and when he said that this was one of the smaller buildings on campus, I almost felt overwhelmed. Like this school would be too much for me to take in, and I started to feel nervous about it. I squeezed Darryl's hand tighter as we went along.

"What do you think so far?" he asked as we trialed behind Mr. Taylor.

"I don't know. It seems kinda big."

"Oh, it is big. This is one of the bigger schools in the D.C. area. I mean, I have a few smaller colleges on the list. Community colleges, you know? Those are the ones that will have a smaller school size, but it is nothing like the true college experience. Living on campus and getting involved in the events that take place here. It is a lot different."

"Yeah. Yeah, I can see that."

"And finally," Mr. Taylor said, "this is the place where the students come to hang out. The Den. Arcade games, bowling alleys, and a mini golf course is just outside. We try to make the campus good enough to where no student has to leave to get what they want. Fast food restaurants are down on the other end of the campus and, like I said, you've only seen less than half of what we have to offer. If I showed you each and every classroom and every building, it would take a few days. So, I just wanted to show you the major attractions."

He smiled and folded his hands in front of him. "So, what do you think of the school, Jae?"

"I like it. I was just telling Darryl how big it was, you know?"

"You should be used to big things," Darryl interjected with a smile.

I closed my eyes and shook my head, hoping that Mr. Taylor didn't pick up on the comment. "So, yeah, I like it. I don't want to make a decision right now because I haven't seen the other schools, but as of now, I do like it."

"Good! Well, as long as you like it and we aren't eliminated from your list, I am good with that. So, we can head back to my office, I can send you home with some more information. Do you think you will need to take out any student loans?"

"Maybe for the first year," Darryl spoke for me. "After

that, I don't think it will be a problem to pay out of pocket."

"Excellent. Well, right this way."

As he walked ahead of us, I spoke to Darryl, "Pay out of pocket next year? What are you talking about? I won't have that kind of money."

"If I go to the league, then I will have that kind of money and if you are my girl, then so will you. So, like I said before, just sit back and let me do this for you. I got you, baby."

It was hard to go against what he said. I took hold of his hand and walked next to him down the hallways and back to Mr. Taylor's office. After he handed me the paperwork, Darryl took me to a few more schools: community colleges and other universities nearby. I felt like a five-star athlete that different schools were trying to woo in their favor. I knew it was all because I was with Darryl though. The special treatment and attention was because they knew he was headed to the NBA. I didn't mind that at all. After everything I saw today, I knew I wanted to go to school. It didn't have to be a fashion school, either, because the one that we visited was not as extensive as the others.

We sat in the car in front of my house. My bag full of brochures and information from all the colleges we visited. "So, what do you think? Is it something that you want to do?"

"Yeah. I think it is something I want to do. College is the next step for me. I should've gone here from the jump so I could avoid all the bullshit I went through in the last year."

"Yeah, but shit happens for a reason. That made you a better and smarter woman and it showed me how much I love you. So, just charge it to the game."

"You're right. It is even better that they took that recording out of rotation after them hoes got charged for the crime. Now, people don't have to look at me and judge me against what they saw on the recording."

"How much time did them hoes get?"

"One year, each. They should've gotten more. Bitches."

As we got out of the car, I thought that maybe I didn't have to keep my choices secluded to whatever was nearby. Maybe I could venture out and find a different college. With the recording banished from social media and everywhere else, I knew I could start fresh anywhere without a care in the world.

CHAPTER 5

Blake

"Do you want anything else to drink, sir?"

"No, James, I am good. Thank you."

The server walked away from me as I sat in the front room with my leg folded over the other, staring at a blank television screen. I hadn't moved in the last hour and I knew James was concerned, but I didn't care. I couldn't remove my mind off what was hanging in front of me. In the blank television screen, my mind always went somewhere that I knew I couldn't be. To a place that didn't exist right now.

In the screen, Jae was seated next to me, underneath my arm. She had her hand on my thigh and we shared laughs with each other while our children ran back and forth across the television. Pretty little versions of both me and her. A little girl with long, jet black hair and a young boy just as curious and rambunctious as his father. That was the world I wanted and it was one that seemed even more fleeting as the time went by. I wanted that life, but I knew I had the wrong woman for the job. Carissa was not made to be anything except for a show wife. I wasn't even sure if she had motherly instincts and that was something that worried me, especially when I thought about any future between us.

Every time I tried to shake the image out of my head, her friend Darryl popped up and I just became even more enraged. I hated that he was there, and I hated even more the thought of him still being there. I couldn't stop my mind from placing them two together in the bed, in the shower and every place me and Jae had been intimate with each other. I wanted to go back over there and break all of it up. She was mine and there was nothing else to say about it.

I grabbed my phone to call her but just like it had been for the past few days, I heard her voicemail instead of her. I ended the call because at this point, I had left enough voicemails and text messages for her to call me back. She was flat out ignoring me and that made me even more upset. I grabbed my keys and headed for the door, but before I could get there, Carissa entered the house.

She forced me to stop in my tracks as she pushed the door closed behind her with a smile on her face. "Hey baby," she said as she put her bags to the side, "I am finally home. Did you miss me?"

Miss you? That was the last thing I expected to hear from her, especially after the way everything went down with me and her over the sex tape. I was sure she would come back fuming, if she came back at all. I even had my lawyer begin to prepare divorce papers just in case she didn't show up. In my mind, I was kind of hoping that she didn't. I was curious to her behavior, though. It made me think she had something else up her sleeve. Paranoia was getting the best of me.

"Why are you so happy?"

"Why shouldn't I be?"

"Because of everything I did while you were gone. All of that stuff with Jae. The tape and everything. The way you acted when I called you and the fact that you have been practically ignoring me ever since then."

"Well, Blake, yes, I was upset. I was upset, but I was also

happy at the fact that you got what you deserved. Now, I know I said I would get you back, but quite frankly, I don't have the mind to concoct anything vindictive like that. It was simply a threat. Not a promise. But, when that happened, in a way, I felt vindicated. So, it is what it is. That doesn't change the fact that I missed you and I am just glad all of that is behind us. It is behind us, right?"

She stepped closer to me. I relaxed the keys in my hand and placed them back on the counter. It wasn't a coincidence that she stopped me just before I went over to Jae's place and caused trouble. Even with that, I couldn't stop thinking about her. "Yeah, I think so. Listen, I want to apologize to you." I took her by the hand and led her over to the couch in the living room.

"About?"

"About everything. The way I have been treating you. Cheating time after time again and not showing you the respect you deserve. Now, I know that we have an agreement. An arrangement, or whatever, but I still haven't been respecting that side of it. I've been doing what I want and in the end, it has made our marriage worse. So, I will take all the blame in that."

She looked away from me. Silence floated between us

for a few moments. "Wow. I um, I guess I am just shocked to hear you say anything like that. I never pegged you as the one who would fess up to any wrong doings like that. It is um, it is sort of shocking to hear you apologize."

"Well, I know what I have done to you is wrong and this time alone has helped me understand that. You deserve more. You deserve better. Like I said, I know what our arrangement is though. You are here for looks and there is really no love between us. I get that, but—"

"No love between us? What do you mean?"

"Our arrangement. You are here for the look. For the feelings, you know? When we go out, I have someone elegant beside me. Someone distinguished and enchanted. You match my aura when we go out and that is what I needed. That is where our relationship stands."

"Wait, so you think I don't love you?"

My eyebrows scrunched together. "No, I don't think you do. How could you? After all I've done? I didn't think it was possible."

She scooted closer to me on the couch. "That is far from the truth, Blake. I do love you. Just because things aren't going the way we imagined does not mean that I don't love you. I am head over heels in love with you."

I couldn't believe what I was hearing. Up until this point, she had made no mention of her loving me in any way. In fact, she barely said anything to me from an emotional standpoint. I didn't understand where she was coming from. "Head over heels? Really?"

"Yes, Blake. Is that so hard to believe?"

"Yes. I mean," I smiled, "I never expected to hear you say that. So, I mean, tell me what it is that you love about me."

"Huh?"

"You love me, so tell me what you love about me."

She stood to her feet and twiddled her fingers together as she paced the room. "I love the way you provide for me. I mean, look at this house. Look at this place. Our cars. I don't have to worry about anything being turned off. Anything getting repossessed or our home being foreclosed on. You take care of it all and you have never allowed me to worry."

I leaned back as she continued, "And you make sure that I have all of my hearts desires. One thing that a man does for his wife is take care of her. He provides for her in every area and the one thing that women want most is security. We want to know that we can come home and not have to worry about bills or anything of that nature."

She looked my way, "And you have done that. You have always done that and that is why it is so hard for me to leave you. You take care of me, Blake. You make sure I am ok. You make sure I am safe. You send me to where I need to go and you don't worry about anything. To me, that is a man. Someone who takes care of home, and takes care of his wife." She leaned forward and kissed me on the lips, but I barely moved to greet her. "That is a man to me. That is why I love you."

I nodded my head as her words lingered in the air. I was hoping that she would say more. Say something about the way I made her feel. The way I treated her. Something that didn't involve the amount of money I made because right now, that seemed to be the only thing that kept her close to me. "So, if I didn't make this amount of money, would you still want to be with me?"

"What? Blake, what kind of question is that?"

"To me, it is a legitimate one. I mean, based on everything you told me."

"So, was this question a set up? The question about whether I loved you or not?"

"A set up? What are you talking about?"

"I gave you my honest answer and you turned it into something else. If I would've known you tried to pull this punch, I would not have entertained you."

"It is just a question, Carissa. Why are you getting upset?"

"I am not getting upset. I just want you to know that I love you and I love you the way I love you. It has nothing to do with materialistic things, but it has everything to do with the way you treat me and if you can't understand that, then we don't have anything else to talk about."

"Carissa—"

"I will be upstairs in the shower. You know, the place where you brought another woman into our home and enjoyed your time with. Yes. That is where I will be if you need me."

I leaned back on the couch and massaged my temples. She had a way of flipping things on me once they got too hot for her. I knew it was coming, but I also knew that she didn't love me the way I needed her to. It was all based on materialistic things and whether she wanted to admit it or not, that was the only reason she loved me. It made me realize that I missed Jae even more. I knew Jae felt stronger about me and it wasn't based on the money. It was based on what we had together. Our chemistry. The way we cared for each other outside of anything materialistic.

I looked at the pictures of her in my phone as I heard the shower water turn on upstairs. I wanted her back now more than ever. I thought about the divorce papers that I had my lawyer begin to draw up. Maybe it would be best to just go through with it and if it meant allowing her to take half of what I owned, then so be it. It would be better to do that than to stay trapped, married to a woman that didn't love me or I had no desire to be with emotionally.

There was no way I could stay married to her under these conditions and the more I thought about Jae, the more I figured I had to make a move. I didn't care who or what was in my way, Jae had to be mine.

CHAPTER 6

Jae

"Oh, shit, you remember this episode of Martin? This the one where Tommy be like, 'I got the draws! I got the draws!' in the courtroom."

He burst out laughing as he laid next to me on the bed. I waived him off as I filled out college applications and worked on essays. Now, I was more focused than I had ever been so I could get into school. I knew that it was my only way out, especially since I couldn't go back to Sugar Baby's. After Erica got arrested, they put the company under her little cousin. From what I heard, they had slowly been losing business because she wasn't as much of a dog as Erica was. She was a little too caring to be in the field and, like Erica, she had to be cutthroat, otherwise, it wouldn't work.

I hadn't heard from Shayla, either, and I didn't expect to. I wanted her to do her time underneath the jail and I couldn't care less if she stayed there for the rest of her life. I hated how she played me and in my mind, she still didn't get what I felt she deserved. "Will you stop rocking back and forth like that? You are making me mess up on this essay."

"Oh. My bad, college girl. I didn't mean to throw you off." He scooted further away as I typed on the keyboard. "Do you need any help?"

"Nah, I got it. You can go ahead and finish watching your Martin re-runs."

He flipped the television off. "Nah, I'm here for you. If you need me, you got me. Just let me know what it is. Do you need someone to look over what you have now? Help you answer some of the questions?"

He grabbed the papers that I printed off and looked through them as I shook my head. "Nah, I got it. Thank you though, bae."

"Damn." He flipped through a few more papers. "I didn't know you did this good on your SAT and ACT.

Shit. You are a borderline fucking genius. You should've been in school or running the country by now. Why didn't you go back then?"

I shrugged my shoulders. "I guess it just wasn't meant for me to go. I mean, it wasn't as clear cut for me as it was for you. You could ball and everybody in the hood could see that you were going to take that talent out of the projects and do something with it. With me? I didn't know my talent. Shit, I still don't. I have to take time to figure that stuff out, but life happened. Shit with my aunt and then I had to figure out how to take care of Angie. I needed to make moves. I didn't have years to waste trying to figure out what I wanted to be in life."

"Damn. Yeah, it was bad back then, but that is why I want to give you the world now. You deserve that. Shit, you deserve more than that. That's why I think you should just skip all this bullshit and come to school with me. Since your life has been so hard in the past, you may as well let me help you take the easy road."

I stroked keys on the keyboard. "No, I don't want the easy road. Anything I get in my hands, I want to earn it. I don't want it handed to me because then, I won't appreciate it. I will feel entitled to that, and anything else that comes my way. I don't want it to be like that."

"Well, if you're going to be with me down the line, that's how it is going to be. You think LeBron's wife has to work? Kobe's? Nah, they don't have to work for shit, and you know why? Because they have been by their man's side through all the bullshit already. The cheating, the not having shit but bread and Kool-Aid to eat, poor as fuck. You know? They been through that and now they are living their best life. It is your turn for that. It is our turn. I want you next to me."

I exhaled and shook my head. Every time he spoke like that, he made me think of Blake. He tried to control me the same way and keep me dependent on him by paying for everything and even trying to pay for my college education. I didn't want that. I had never allowed a man to run me in that way and I didn't want to begin. Not after all I had been through. "Nah, I'm good. I want to make my own way, Darryl. I don't want to benefit off what you have already started. Just let me do this on my own. That's what's wrong with yall men. Yall want to come in and try to control everything. Just let a flower grow on its own. Water me with love and attention and watch me grow."

"Hold on." He sat upright on the edge of the bed. "Control you? I have never tried to control you. What are you talking about?"

"You are trying to control me now, Darryl."

"No, I'm not. You know that's not how I move." He stood up and shook his head. "Is that what Blake did? Is that what he tried to do? Control you?" I sucked my teeth as he continued, "Nah, don't try to act like I'm pulling this shit out of my ass because I'm not. I've picked up on yo' lil' comments over the days. You say stuff that I haven't done and I know you are just takin' shit out on me that that fuck nigga did to you. I'm not him. I am yo' man, not some fuckin' nigga payin' you for your time. I am not payin' you to fu—"

I cut my eyes at him. I knew what he was about to say and I could feel his words on the edge of his tongue. It didn't matter that he cut it short because the words had already cut my heart. "Are you fucking serious right now?"

"Jae, I didn't mean—"

"I kept it a buck with you about Blake and everything and you are just going to throw it back in my face like that? For real? Use it against me in an argument the first time you can?" I moved my laptop to the side and stood to my feet, "you know what? Maybe we are moving too fast. Maybe we shouldn't be in a relationship with each other until you can get over what I did in my past because I'm not about to keep lettin' you throw this shit back in my face. I already had enough of it each time I stepped outside, Darryl!"

I started for the door, but he quickly moved in front of me, keeping me away from the handle. I shoved him backwards into the door. "Move! Don't touch me! I already had enough of that shit! Going out in public. People pointing their finger at me because of that fuckin' sex tape! You don't think I've been embarrassed enough? You think I want to hear that shit from you?"

"Listen, I'm sorry, Jae. I didn't mean to offend you like that, but I just wanted you to know that I'm not like him. I'm nothing like Blake and you keep comparing me to him and making me pay for the shit he did to you. That ain't right, Jae."

"You know what else ain't right? This." He tilted his head to the side. "The way you come and go in my life and expect shit to flow the way you want it to when you show up again. Do I look like a fucking coat that you can pick up and put on when you want to? Huh? What happens when you get tired of me again? What happens when I piss you off again? Are you going to walk away and leave me in the dark for months at a time? Weeks?

Years? Huh? Because I don't have time for that shit, Darryl!"

He stepped closer to me and grabbed my arms. "Let me the fuck go, Darryl!"

I snatched out of his grasp as he stood in front of me, quietly. My chest moved up and down from anger as I panted in front of him. He shoved his hands in his pockets and leaned against the door. Tears silently rolled down my cheeks. I loved him, but I hated how things had been going between us. I knew it would just take something small to set either of us off, and after that, it was back to the status quo. He would leave for some time and not come back or I would block him out of my life. That is the only thing that made me unsure about him. The consistency. The consistency between us. It scared the shit out of me.

"Baby, I'm sorry, aight? I'm sorry. I know you don't want to hear that right now." I plopped down onto the bed. "But I am and there is nothing else I can do or say to erase what I was about to say earlier. I was just upset, aight?"

"You don't cut me with your words when you are mad! I am not some little side chick that you can talk to however you want to talk to!"

"I know, I know." He eased down beside me, "I know. You are much more than that to me. You are not just some side chick. You are my only one. You are the one I want to spend the rest of my life with and I've known it since I was a kid. Since those nights we laid together in bed, holding each other until Angie got home. The times when all we had were each other. I miss that shit, but I know that is the shit that kept me close to you. That made me understand that there was nobody else in the world like you. I need you, baby. I don't think less of you for what you did. I love you for how you have persevered through it all. I'm sorry."

I sat on the edge of the bed. I didn't want to accept what he said because I was still upset. I knew he wouldn't just get over what I did and I couldn't blame him for it. I understood. If he made a sex tape, I don't even know if I would ever get over it, so I had to respect him from that point of view. I used my hand to wipe a tear from the bottom of my eye, then stood to my feet to grab a piece of Kleenex out of the box.

I watched him in the mirror as he stayed seated, looking off to the right. I loved him and there was no doubt about it, but I was just unsure if we would be able to last because of our history. Normally, history is what would keep two people together, not break them apart. I thought about Blake for a moment, wondering if the fact that we didn't have a past could help our future. But there was no way that he could replace the way Darryl made me feel. The comfort. The peace. The relaxation. There was no comparison.

"I'ma go in here and get something to eat. I just need a minute, ok?"

"A minute for what?"

"Just to think, ok, Darryl? That's all. I just need to think."

He exhaled, then leaned backwards on the bed until he faced the ceiling. I walked out of the room and closed the door behind me. I didn't know what was going to happen between us from here and quite frankly, I was scared to death of losing him.

CHAPTER 7

"Ok, what the hell is wrong with yall? Yall been actin funny since I came in the front room. Ain't sayin' nothin' to each other. Walkin' by with cold shoulders. What the fuck happened yesterday because yall wasn't like this before I left."

I sat in the kitchen with my plate of eggs and biscuits in front of me as Darryl walked to the stove. I knew he was looking for his food, but he must've been crazy if he thought I was going to fix him anything after that shit he said last night. He sucked his teeth, then went to the cabinet and pulled a box of cereal out. "People just wanna' be petty, Angie. That's all it is."

"Nah, people are just so spoiled and used to gettin' everything they want and talkin' to people any kind of way that they think they can do it to anybody."

"Ain't nobody talkin' any kind of way to nobody."

I scrunched my face together. "Um, Angie? Did you hear somebody talking? Because it sounds like somebody might be outside or somethin'. I don't know. Can you check?"

"See, that is exactly what I'm talkin' about. Petty as fuck."

He slammed the box of cereal down, then walked out of the kitchen, leaving the two of us alone. I dug my fork into the mound of eggs and pushed it to my mouth as Angie sat down in the chair beside me. "Really? I mean, seriously, what the fuck happened? What yall do? It can't be too bad if he still here and you ain't left to go nowhere."

I finished my food, then stood up to take my plate to the sink. "He just don't know how to control his tongue. That's all. He thinks I am one of the little hoes he messes with on campus. I ain't none of them lil' broads out there. He got me fucked up."

"What he say?"

I put my plate in the sink and then put my hands on the edge of the counter. I hated thinking about it. His words sent my stomach turning into knots. "He just knows how to hurt me, that's all. I know he didn't do it on purpose, but he still did it. I mean, said it. I just don't want to talk about it though."

"Shit, well, something gotta change because we are going out to see aunt Jeanie today and she don't need to see yall arguing with each other or going back and forth with the cold shoulders. Yall need to fix this shit before we get there. For real."

She stood up, then went to her room so she could get dressed. I shrugged my shoulders, then washed out my plate and started to put Darryl's box of cereal back in the cabinet, but I stopped myself. *Fuck that. I ain't doin' shit for that nigga; he can come and put up his own damn box of cereal.* I slammed the box on the counter, then went to my room to get dressed and ready to go see aunt Jeanie.

Angie climbed into the driver's seat. I sat in the front and Darryl slid his way into the back. Angie started the engine and with that, we were on our way. We drove with the music up for a few minutes before she turned it down. "Look, I don't know what the fuck is goin' on with yall, but if yall make me act like the mama, then got damnit, I will! Is somebody going to tell me what is going on? Or am I gon' have to turn this car back around and go home."

"Girl, please, you ain't takin' us home. Stop playin'."

"Then, you need to tell me what is wrong. Both of yall." We didn't say a word as she continued down the street. After she realized we weren't going to say anything to her, she spoke up. "Well, fuck it. If yall are gon' be stubborn about this shit, then fine. But, yall can't take this out here to aunt Jeanie. She is in rehab and she doesn't need to see any beef between yall two or anybody else. We need to keep this shit positive, so, if yall won't do it for me, then please, do it for her."

She was right. We didn't need bring our drama out to the rehab spot with aunt Jeanie because she would pick up on it and it could change her mood. I folded my arms over my chest. "Aight, fine. I will agree to a truce while we are here if that sucka in the back will agree too it, too."

"What? See, that's what I'm sayin', Angie, she always got somethin' slick to say! I didn't even say shit to her!"

"You said enough shit last night, nigga!"

"Ok, ok! Damn! Aight, so, is there gon' be a truce or not

because I was serious about going back home. If yall are gon stay like this, then yall can drive out there another time and I'll go by myself to see aunt Jeanie. Think I'm playin'. Is this gon' be a truce or not?"

I shrugged my shoulders. "I said yeah. It's on him."

"Fine. A fuckin' truce for now. But we will finish this shit later."

"I don't give a damn what yall do later as long as yall don't do it now. Shit. Both of yall some petty mutha-fuckas. Got damn. Yall are perfect for each other."

I lifted one eyebrow above the other, then turned the volume up on the music so I could drown out anything else that Darryl tried to say. As far as I was concerned, this was for aunt Jeanie and her only. I slid my earbuds in and listened to my music the rest of the ride there.

When I woke up, Angie was just pulling into the rehab center. I rubbed my eyes and caught the end of her and Darryl's conversation. "Yeah, that was crazy. You came up there, swole as fuck, like, 'who was out here messin' with my sister!'" She laughed. "You had them little boys scared as fuck."

"Hell yeah, I remember that. I am serious about mine

though. I will go to war for you, sis. Them little niggas was about to catch these hands, on everything."

"I know, bro. Trust me, I know."

"What are yall talkin' about?"

"We talkin' about that time Angie came in to get me because some dudes was messin' with her outside yall apartment in the projects. Them niggas thought it was sweet until I came out there with that bat."

I laughed to myself, recalling the story they told me about years ago. They had such a tight relationship between them that I found it hard to believe they were never intimate with each other. They seemed like a better fit, but I could tell that they were just brothers and sisters. That was the relationship they had and I could never imagine a different kind of vibe between them.

"Ok, here we are. I feel bad as shit that I haven't been to visit her since we dropped her off. You think she mad?"

"I hope she isn't. I mean, it was a lot of shit going on back home though. I called and talked to her though, so she wasn't just out in the dark."

"Yeah, I called and talked to her, too, but that ain't the same as a visit."

"Well, I had a legit reason," Darryl said as he reached for the door handle. "I was away at college, so, I'ma be watching while she snap on yall asses."

I shook my head and got out of the car, then the three of us made our way to the entrance of the building. Things hadn't changed much since we came the last time. The landscaping was beautiful as the sun reflected the fresh cut blades of grass in the front lawn. "Shit, all of this money, I hope that my auntie looks as good as this front yard. Shit."

We headed inside and to the front desk. A lady greeted us with a smile and after we told her who we came to see, she pointed us in the right direction and we were off. We slowly approached the door and pulled it open. Aunt Jeanie smiled as soon as she saw us and for a moment, I didn't believe it was her because she looked nothing like she did when we dropped her off.

Her hair had grown and stretched down the middle of her back in a grey and black mix of beauty. Her natural brown complexion returned to her body and the blemishes in her skin were non-existent. Tears rushed to my eyes and stopped at the edge while Angie ran and threw her arms around her neck. "Aunt Jeanie! You look amazing, auntie! Oh, my God!"

I stood there with my hands covering my mouth. Now it all made sense. I hated working for Sugar Baby, but now that I saw what it did for my aunt. What I was able to get her for going through what I went though, it made it all worth it. The pain, the drama and suffering was all worth it if I got to see my aunt in her regular state of mind.

"Darryl? Is that you?"

"Yes, ma'am."

"My goodness, you have shot straight to ceiling. Come on over here and give me a hug, boy!"

He walked towards her and as the two embraced, Angie stood to the side, wiping tears from her cheeks. We shared the same joy because we both knew the same sorrows. The days she came home high as hell, trying to steal things out of our place just to get her next fix. We had been through it all and to see her like this was nothing short of a miracle.

"Ok, Jae, it is your turn now. Come on over here and give your auntie a hug."

I sniffled, then slow walked to her. She wrapped her arms around me. She smelled like peppermint and fresh body wash. Something that I hadn't smelled on her in ages. She felt like my aunt. She felt like my flesh and blood and I couldn't get any words out without crying first. I held onto her for what seemed like hours until we released each other.

She held my hand and wiped tears off her cheeks with the other. She took a deep breath, then exhaled. "I am so happy to see yall. I am so glad that yall came out here. It wasn't as much as yall said yall would come, but I understood that you all had things you had to take care of." She looked at Angie, still smiling. "Ang told me that she decided to go to school and that now, you are considering it. Is that right?"

I nodded my head. She smiled harder. "I am so proud of you both! You two will go so much further than what I did in my life and I can't wait to see you two on top of the world. On top of it all!" We paused for a few moments. I still couldn't find the words to say to her. Suddenly, she led me over to the wall. "Let me show you what I've done since I've been here. Now, it has been tough at times, you know, the withdrawal that I deal with. But the counselors here are amazing. They helped me redirect my passion and addiction to something else."

She showed me the artwork that hung on her walls. Complex, ambiguous pieces of art that she was enamored by. "They gave me a paintbrush and told me to use it whenever I got the urge to hold a joint or a pipe. I didn't make sense at first. At times, I took that paint brush and hauled it across the room, but they just walked over, picked it up and put it back on my tray. After I realized they weren't going anywhere and there was no way that I could get a high, I started painting."

She showed me another piece of work. "At first, it was dark and ugly things. Almost like I was painting the worst side of me, you know? Painting the demons that tormented me and my addiction. It was like that for a few weeks, but after that, they changed. They became brighter and my addictions lessened. Now, it's totally different. Now, I look forward to painting and I really feel like I have found my calling."

"These are amazing, aunt Jeanie. For real. I am impressed," Angie said from the side.

"Yes, that's what they all say up here. They said I missed my calling, but to me? I didn't miss it. Artists are much older than me, still putting out great work. I think I still have time to do it. I think I still have time."

"You do, aunt Jeanie," Darryl added. "I believe in you. This stuff is really good."

"Thank you, Darryl." I could feel her eyes on me and moments later, she asked if Darryl and Angie could give us a minute alone.

They stayed in the room while she took me outside. We walked down the hallway and through the front doors. About twenty yards out in the front, we sat down in front of a large, angelic statue. She sat down on the bench in front of it, then extended her hand for me to sit next to her. She put her hand in mine and took a deep breath. "You know, it took me a long time to come to this place mentally. Where I am now. And, like I was telling you before about the painting, I had to face my demons before I was able to do anything."

She looked directly into my eyes as a soft breeze blew against us. "And, there was one thing in particular that I had to face. Something that has caused me shame since the days I allowed it to happen. That stuff with Melvin—"

"Aunt Jeanie, that is—"

"No, no. You have to let me say this sweetheart, ok? I've worked up to this point because I knew it had to happen and if I don't do this, then I will just bury it inside of me and let it make my heart rotten once again. I can't do that. I have to let this out, ok? Will you let me?"

I nodded my head. She took another deep breath, then looked ahead at the angel while holding my hand, and continued, "I am sorry that I didn't believe you back then. I should've taken your word over his about him touching on you, but I didn't. I know it is not an excuse, but I blame it on the drugs. They really had me messed up mentally back then and like I said, it is not an excuse because nothing can excuse my disgusting behavior. Nothing at all, but I am sorry. I am truly sorry and I hope that you can forgive me."

I tried to hold back my tears, but it was no use. They flooded out of my eyes, one after the other, as I thought back to the times Melvin put his hands on me and I begged him to stop. I begged aunt Jeanie to listen to me, but she never did, and it kept happening. I tried to forget all of that and bury it away, but it found its way back up, so I had to face it. There was no way around it.

She grabbed my hand tighter. "Baby, if you can't find it to forgive me, I understand. I completely understand because that is not something easy to forget or get over. That is not something that I expect you to just snap your fingers and forgive because I know it is tough. It took me a long time to even be able to face myself about this issue. So, please take as much time as you need to. You don't have to say anything about it now, but I just wanted you to know that—I remember—and I am sorry. I am sorry from the depths of my heart, ok sweetheart?"

I couldn't say anything back to her. With tears rolling out of my eyes, I wrapped my arms around her and hugged her as tightly as I could. I could feel that she wasn't the same woman back then and I understood how drugs could have an effect on what she did and how she behaved. It was the reason why I wanted her to get help.

After we released, she wiped tears from under my eyes, then stood to her feet. "Well, we can go back inside now. That is, unless you have something you need to say."

I shook my head. I wasn't ready to say anything about that yet. I just needed to process everything and make sure that I was healed from it all, but the fact that she apologized was good enough for me. I knew that between us, I could finally close that chapter in my life.

We stayed out there with her for a few more hours

before we decided to take off. "Now, don't let that much time go by before yall come back to see me, ok?"

"Yes, ma'am," I said as we all hugged her one by one.

After we got in the car, I told Angie and Darryl what she said to me out in the front yard. Angie started crying and shortly after that, Darryl had to convince her to pull over so he could finish driving the rest of the way. Nobody said a word for the remainder of the ride.

CHAPTER 8

We hadn't spoken much at all since we came back from visiting aunt Jeanie. I was still upset with Darryl, but it wasn't as nearly as much as before. The trip helped me see what was most important and even though I wanted to be mad at him and keep holding a grudge, I knew that It was pointless. I looked at him as he sat in the bed, flipping through channels on the television.

"Is Martin on?"

"Nah, I don't think so. Why?"

"Because I remember how we used to watch that together back in the day. I was just hoping that it was on, you know? For nostalgia's sake."

"Oh. Well, nah, it ain't on."

He flipped through the channels as I stood in front of the dresser. Moments later, I walked over to him and took the remote out of his hands, looking him into his eyes. "You aight?"

"I'm better than I was. Listen, I just want to apologize for acting like a bitch earlier and everything. I was just upset and you know how I can get. Holding onto things, you know?"

"Yeah, I know. I know exactly how you are, but I didn't want this to be how it normally is between us. I get mad and leave or you get mad and ignore me. I mean, you still ignored me, but I'm usually gone, so it doesn't matter. I wanted to stop handling things that way because I knew it wouldn't help us in the long run."

"Yeah, you're right. It wouldn't. I know you love me and honestly, I love you, too. You know that. Or, if you don't, I hope you do now. I was just being stubborn and I did allow my past relationships to effect how things were going between us. So, I am sorry. I am going to try not to do that."

"I get it though. You gotta' make your own way. You don't have to follow me at my school or anything and I respect that. I gotta' respect that. I guess I was just being selfish and trying to get what I want, no matter what. That's not how this works and I get it."

"I guess we both made some mistakes. You know, this whole 'gettin' with yo' best friend' thing is a little more complicated than they wanted us to believe."

"Yeah, but it is easier in the end. We know each other well. I know what to do when you get mad and you know what to do when I get mad. It is best for us to have that kind of relationship, you know? At least, that is what I think."

"You are right."

I crawled into his arms and wrapped my arms around his body. I only thought about Blake a few times over the past few days. He called me, but I didn't think it was fair to him or Darryl to answer. I knew he just wanted to check on me and see how I was doing, but there was nothing left between us. I knew Darryl was the one for me and it didn't make sense to give Blake any more attention. Besides that, I didn't want to explain to Darryl who I was talking to. If I was going to leave my past in the past, that meant leaving Blake there as well.

"So, we have wasted what? Like a day of time because

we both wanted to be mad at each other. We gotta make up for that."

"Yeah, we do. So, what do you want to do?"

"I don't know. Well, I know one thing we can do? You know, they say the best park of getting mad at each other is the part where you make up."

"Make up? What? Say how sorry we are and then have prayer?"

"What?" he said, laughing. "I mean, there is nothing wrong with prayer, but that is not exactly what I had in mind."

"Well, Darryl..." I ran my finger on the edge of his lips. "What exactly did you have in mind?"

He smiled, then slid his hands down to my backside. I scooted up into his arms until I straddled his hips with my arms around his neck. "I got a few things in mind. Maybe you can help me out with it?"

"Maybe?" I kissed him on the lips. "I'm thinking that won't be a problem at all."

He grabbed the sides of my face and pulled me in for a kiss, quenching the flame of my anger in a moment's time. His tongue danced inside of my mouth as my guards went down. His hand slid onto my backside. My breathing intensified. My heart pounded inside my chest as he laid me down on the mattress.

His lips pressed against mine softly as he slid my pants down below my waist. *Thank God I shaved today*, I thought as he moved his head towards my vagina. I felt his tongue caress the outside of my vagina as I leaned my head back onto the mattress. He propped my thighs over his shoulders as he buried his head further between them, gripping onto the top of my legs to keep me in place. Gentle strokes brushed against my clitoris as I bit my lip and grabbed a handful of my breasts as my nipples stiffened like Hershey kisses and jabbed the palm of my hand.

Three more strokes with his tongue sent my legs into convulsions and contracted my thighs around his neck. He moved his head around in a circular motion, licking every inch of my cat as I grabbed the back of his head to keep him steady when he hit my spot. "Right there, baby, right there. Don't stop." He sucked on my clit and used his finger to press inside of my vagina, and as I fixed my mouth to utter pleasure, nothing came out. My legs shook as a tidal wave spilled from my vagina and into his mouth as he slurped everything that came out. My breathing increased as he reached his hand up and squeezed my tender breast. He licked me slowly until I was finished, then he stood up and reached for a towel to wipe his mouth.

A few moments of silence passed as we sat inches away from each other. I closed the gap between us and locked my lips with his again. This time, I wasn't going to stop. I put my hand on the side of his face and climbed on top of him. I straddled his waist with our lips intertwined like strands of DNA. With one hand, he grabbed my backside and guided me closer to him. I leaned my head back as his tongue danced down the middle of my neck until he met with my breasts. I pulled my shirt from over my head and tossed it to the side.

I reached behind and unstrapped my bra, releasing my breasts from their momentary prison. He wrapped his lips around my nipples, twirling them in his mouth like a lollipop before he suctioned my breast. I bit my lip as I held the back of his head. I could feel him rising beneath me, poking the outer portion of my undergarments. He shifted his attention to my other breast as heavy, passionate breaths escaped my lungs in bursts of ecstasy. My panties were soaked, and my mind was conflicted as we danced together in flames of hell.

I squatted over him, so I could unbuckle his pants. He

yanked his pants down to his ankles, then his underwear followed right after. His dick shot straight up like an exclamation mark. My vagina dripped onto the tip of it as I gazed into his lonely eyes. It looked as though he found his way out through me. The desperation in his eyes spoke volumes as I lowered myself onto his penis. The tip of it cracked my vagina as I eased down onto him. His dick burst through my pussy lips like a snake forcing its way into a rabbit hole. I fixed my mouth to utter moans of pleasure, but nothing escaped.

He put his hand on my shoulder and pushed me down further as he exhaled passionate groans. My lips fit tight around his dick, and at that moment, I felt his head climb to chambers in my vagina that hadn't been touched in years. I bounced up and down on top of him. My titties moved like basketballs as I dug my nails into the back of his neck. His chest glistened with sweat as he leaned his head on the back cushion of the couch. He grabbed hold of my waist with his hand and guided me back and forth on top of him, smacking my behind as I moved according to his command. Suddenly, he grabbed my neck and pulled me in. His lips had pressed against mine moments before he stood up with my legs wrapped around his waist like a boa constrictor.

He dropped me on the bed, then mounted me as he

forced my legs back behind my head until they made a V-shape. His muscles contracted as he pushed himself deeper inside of me. I screamed out of pleasure and pain as I dug my nails into his back. My body bounced up and down on the mattress. His hands slid around my throat, choking me delicately, but forcefully enough to know that he could end my life at any moment if he wanted to. The passion drove me up a wall as his muscular frame hoovered over me like a spaceship. His dick slid in and out of me like a groundhog checking for his shadow. "Shit," I yelled out, "shit!" I could feel myself building up for a release. My pussy lips pulsated as sweat dripped from his muscular chest.

"Kiss me!" I said, pulling him closer to me. As his tongue swam around in my mouth, a tidal wave flooded from my vagina and exploded onto his dick like a stick of dynamite. I screamed out in ecstasy, my voice bouncing off the walls in the front room. He moaned, and just moments later, I felt his dick pulsating inside of me. His eyes rolled to the back of his head as he yelled out obscenities. His words mingled together with my screams as we shared the same pleasure and minutes later, his bare chest relaxed on top of me as he laid between my legs.

"Baby, I was thinking about something."

"About what?" I asked as I tried to catch my breath.

"I was thinking that—if I asked you to marry me, what would you say? I mean, not that we have to get married any time soon or anything like that because I know I am finishing school and you are trying to get started. But, hypothetically, you know? If I were to ask you, what would you say?"

I had thought about this scenario many times and in my mind, it always played out different. Sometimes, I would smile and say yes, then leap into his arms like they did in all of the movies and in others, I would tell him no with tears falling from my eyes as I watched him walk out of my life for good. Those were the times that I was still involved with Blake, so I knew that was why those imag-inations turned out the way the did. It wasn't like that now, and I knew Darryl was the one.

"I would say yes. Without a doubt, I would say yes."

He held me closer and in moments, I drifted off to sleep.

CHAPTER 9

Darryl

"Angie, you up?"

"What?"

"Are you up?"

"No, nigga. The lights are out and it is dark as hell in here. What do you mean, am I up?"

I went into her room and closed the door behind me, then flipped on her bedroom light. "Good, well, since you're up, I need some help."

"Darryl, what the fuck?" She grabbed her phone and looked at the time. "It is 4 o'clock in the morning. What the hell do you have to talk to me about this early? And with that bright ass light on! Turn it off!"

"Yo', aight, if I turn it off, you gotta' promise me that you won't fall back to sleep."

"Darryl, turn the fuckin' light off." I flipped it off, then used my phone to move around her room until I found the edge of the bed. "Nigga, what do you want? And this better be good. I got fuckin' class later today."

"Yo', I think I want to propose to Jae."

"What?"

"I said I think I want to propose to Jae. I mean, I don't have a lot of money to get her the ring I want to get her. A ring I know she deserves, but I want to make it official. I need some help with that."

She sat upright in her bed and leaned against the head-rest. "Are you serious?"

"Yes. I am dead ass right now. I know I want to finish my life with her by my side. I can't imagine it any other way."

"Oh, my God, Darryl! Yes!" She leaned forward and wrapped her arms around me, nearly squeezing the life out of my body. "Yes! Finally, you are really going to be my fuckin' brother! It is about time you grew some balls and did it, you fuckin' punk!"

"Shut up, Angie! Got damn! But yo', like I said, I just came in here because I need some help. I don't know where to go to get a ring or where to propose or none of that shit. Can you help me?"

"Well, shit, you can go to the pawn shop and get a decent engagement ring for a couple hundred dollars. That shit in there is real and it is cheap. Muhfuckas mad because they man cheated on them or whatever and they just want to pawn that shit. So, check there. You remember the one downtown on 7th?" I nodded my head. "Aight. Yeah, go there."

"Aight, I'ma check that out. But, I don't know where to propose. I've been laying in there with her thinking about it all night."

"Wait, you told her about it already?"

I shook my head. "No, Angie. What the fuck? Why would I tell her about it?"

"Shit, I don't know. It's early and my mind ain't thinking right. Anyways," she got excited, "oh, I know where you can take her! Take her down to the Washington monument. You remember when we used to take the train down there when we were younger and we would all just sit and look at the tourists while they took pictures, thinking—"

"About how they knew nothing about what D.C. was really like? They just came there to snap pictures and then go on with their lives, wherever they came from. Yeah. I remember that good. I used to get mad about it, but then, I just used it to help me focus. I used it as a driving force to make sure I did what I had to do to get the fuck up out of the hood."

"Yup. And Jae felt the same way. That's why she did what she did. You know, working for sugar baby. She just wanted to make money and get us up out the hood and never look back. I know that if you take her there, she would love it. It would be so nostalgic for her. She is going to cry. I know she is."

"Cool, the Washington monument then. I'ma take her there. And, I know you said you had class today, but—"

"Shit, I can miss a class. I haven't missed one yet and if you think I'm not going to see my sister get engaged to my brother, then you must not know who I am. I will be there recording, yelling and doing everything I can to draw attention to yall." She clapped her hands together.

"This is going to be so special! Oh, my God, I don't think I will be able to go back to sleep."

I stood up. "Yo', you better not let this slip out, Angie. I swear on everything we gon' have problems if you accidentally tell her."

"Boy, shut up and just go get the ring before I punch you in the face."

I smiled, then leaned in and hugged her. After that, I went back to the room and got dressed. The pawn shop opened at 8 am, so I had a little time before I had to leave. I went into the kitchen and cooked breakfast for them, then left it in the oven with a note on top of the table.

Afterwards, I went down to the pawn shop to look for a ring. Angie was right. There were a lot of choices within my budget. I figured I would upgrade her as soon as I stepped into the league or started making money in my career field. Either way, she was going to have the princess cut diamond that she always talked about.

After I checked out of the store, I headed back to the crib. Jae and Angie were already up, eating the breakfast I prepared for them. "Hey, babe," Jae said as I walked through the door and into the kitchen. "Where did you go this morning?"

"I went to go check on a few more colleges for you just so you could have more options."

"More options? Baby, I already have enough as it is, and you want to give me more?"

"You can never have too many, or be too particular when it comes to your education. So, yeah, I just wanted to make sure you had all you needed."

"Oh. Ok. Well, thanks for being proactive, sweetie. That was so thoughtful of you." Angie smiled as she looked back and forth between us. Jae turned just as she saw her sister's smile stretch from ear-to-ear. "And what the hell are you cheesing for?"

"Because I am happy to see you two back on speaking terms with each other. It is such a beautiful thing."

"Uh, ok," she said, rolling her eyes. "And I still don't know why you made me get dressed this early. Where are we going? And don't you have class later today?"

"I want to take yall somewhere," I said, interrupting her. "I mean, my spring break is coming to an end and, like I said, I want to make up for the day that we wasted mad at each other. We ruined Angie's day, too, so I think she should be included."

"But I don't think she should be missing classes just to kick it."

"Girl, please. I'll be fine. I haven't missed a day and half the class has already missed one or two by now. I am fine." She stood up. "So, Darryl, where are you taking us?"

"I figured we could catch the train and go down to the Washington monument, you know? Like old days. Reminisce about how far we have come."

Jae smiled. "Aww, that is so sweet, Darryl. I mean, I still don't think Angie should miss school for that, but alright. If she wants to go, then I am fine with going. I think it would be cool."

"Aight, cool. Go and get your purse and we will be out here waiting. Oh, and don't worry about your plate. I put that in the sink and clean it up for you."

She stood up and kissed me on the lips. "Thank you, baby."

I waited until she left the kitchen, then grabbed her plate and took it to the sink. Angie quickly rushed to my side. "Let me see the ring," she said in a hushed tone.

"Sssssh! Damn, she is going to hear you," I hissed back at her.

"Shut up and just let me see the ring! Hurry up before she comes back!" I put the plate in the sink, then quickly took it out of my pocket. Her eyes widened as she looked at it. "My God, that is beautiful. You got that at the pawn shop?"

"Yeah. I was surprised it was there, but I took it. It was only $400, too."

"Damn, that's it? Shit, I need to go up there and see what else they got. And they had her size?"

"Yup. Like it was meant to be."

She slapped hands with me. "Oh shit, here she comes! Put it up!"

I took it from her, shoved it into my pocket and then turned on the sink to wash out her plate. "So, you ready?" Angie asked as she walked over to her.

"Yeah, I'm ready whenever yall are."

I put the plate in the drain and with that, we all walked

out the door and headed for the train. I held her hand as the soft breeze blew against us. "Man, this is exactly how we used to kick it back in the day. The three amigos."

Angie laughed. "Hell yeah. We were the original migos. Fuck Offset, Onset and Goset or whatever the fuck they names is."

We laughed along with her as we climbed into the train and headed downtown. I couldn't stop gazing into Jae's eyes, imagining what life would be like further down the line for us. Pretty little girls that looked just like her. That is what I wanted and that is what I dreamed of. I couldn't wait for it to happen. Finally, the train arrived at our spot. We stepped off and walked down to the monument, holding hands, while Angie strayed behind us, snapping pictures.

"Um, what is paparazzi doing back there?" Jae asked, looking at Angie.

"Shut up! These are memories for me! Yall are my two favorite people in the world and I love it when yall are happy. So, just shut up and be happy!"

She snapped more pictures as we stood in front of the monument. While Angie had her attention, I dropped down to one knee and pulled the ring out of my pocket. I opened the case and waited for her to turn around. She laughed, then tried to walk forward, but stumbled over me. "Darryl, what are you—"

She froze once she saw me kneeled before her. She put her hand over her heart and laughed, "Boy, stop playin' with me. You play too much. Get up off the ground in front of all these people." I didn't budge. I kept the ring in front of her with a smile on my face. "Boy, get up," she said, laughing nervously, "you are not about to make me think you are proposing to me just so this can be some funny little prank. I knew Angie was back there recording for a reason! I don't have time for yall games! Darryl, get up!"

"Baby, I've known from the day we used to talk all night in each other's arms and never do anything else, that you were the one for me." She put her hand over her mouth. "I can't imagine myself with anyone else, and I don't want to. I don't want anybody else to wear my last name. I don't want to start a family with anyone else. You are the alpha and the omega of me. The beginning, the end and you have been everything in between. You are my life and I would love it if you would spend the rest of your life with me."

With tears in her eyes, she nodded her head, then kneeled on the cement with me as we hugged each other. "Yes! Yes! Everybody, my brother just proposed to my sister! Yes!" She paused. "Wait a minute, that shit sounded weird as fuck. One of my best friends just proposed to my sister and he is about to be my brother! Aye yall, congratulate them! You with the long ass face, congratulate my sister and my brother to be!"

We continued embracing each other as Angie made a scene in front of us and drew a small crowd. They all clapped and cheered us on. I couldn't imagine it going any other way between us.

CHAPTER 10

Blake

I stood outside, watching Jae in the arms of Darryl. My heart fell out of my chest and broke into pieces beneath me. I couldn't believe that another man had swooped in and took her right from under me. I didn't move fast enough. I should've just ended things with Carissa when she mentioned it, but instead, I gambled. I took a chance, thinking she would always be there. Believing, in my haughty state of mind, that no other man would be able to come in and provide for her the way that I had in the past.

That was my mistake. I took her for granted and now, it was too late. I looked down in my hand. I held the paper that outlined the details of my divorce with Carissa. It was hell bringing it to her, but once she understood that she would have half of everything, she relaxed and immediately told me to fuck off. It was better that it happened that way instead of us going along with each other, pretending to be something that we weren't. But now, it seemed like it was all for naught.

People gathered around them as they held each other, taking pictures and congratulating them on their engagement. A part of me wanted to go down there and interrupt them. Have my men rough Darryl up and teach him a lesson about touching another man's property. My hands balled into fist at the end of my arms as I watched the two of them hold each other while her sister snapped pictures.

I took the paper and crumbled it up in my hand, then tossed it to the side. I knew that wouldn't have been enough. Not now. A piece of paper outlining the divorce was nothing like official divorce papers being signed and final. I had to wait to bring that to her because our lawyers weren't done sorting out all of my property and materials.

"You want us to go down there, Blake?" one of my security guards as he stood off to the side.

"No. No, just let them be for now. I have to figure out a

better way to go about this. She is making a wrong choice and she knows it. She has to know it. It wouldn't make sense for her to fall into the arms of another man, especially after she tasted what I could do for her. It is nonsense, but, if you go down there now and hurt him, she will never forgive me and it will ruin my chances."

I glared at Darryl. Tall, handsome and seemingly with a past that I couldn't compare to. They had history with each other and that would sustain them over anything that she and I built over the time she was my sugar baby. I had to figure out some kind of way to interrupt their connection. Break it off before it had the chance to develop into something more serious than it was. Engagements could be broken off. It happens all the time and this would be no different.

Just then, the lightbulb went off in my mind. "That is it. We can dig around in his past. I have the means to do it and money long enough to expose everything he did in the past. Maybe I can dig up an old relationship and forge some type of unfaithfulness between the two of them. That will send her right back into my arms. A man like him? I am sure he has a trail of scorned women behind him that would love nothing but to break up their little happy home. And, if not, they have a price. They all have a price. I can give them whatever they want just so long as they stick to the story I concoct. What do you think?"

My guard nodded his head. "That sounds like a plan, boss. Do you want me to call Charles and get him started?"

"No. No, not yet. I need a little more information because I only know his first name. Well, I guess Charles can figure that out. His name is Darryl." I glared at the two of them as they held hands and started walking around the monument, smiling with each other. "That is all I have, but Charles is paid to find things beneath the surface. Call him and let him know to get on it."

"Ok. But, if you don't want to be seen, then we should go before they make their way around here."

"Yes, you are right. Ok. Let's go."

My guard started to walk away, and I lingered just long enough to see them embrace each other again. It drove me crazy the way he held her. The way he kissed her as he stroked her hair with his hands. That was my woman, and sooner or later, he was going to realize that he messed with the wrong person. I would teach him the hard way not to step onto another man's property unless he was ready to deal with the consequences. I climbed into the back seat of my Maybach and headed home. I was ready for war and he had no idea what was about to come his way.

Find out what happens next in the next installment of Secrets Of A Sugar Baby! Coming Soon!

Follow Mia Black on Instagram for more updates: @authormiablack

ALSO BY MIA BLACK

Loved this series so far? Make sure you check out more of Mia Black's series listed below:

Love On The Low

Loving The Wrong Man

When You Can't Let Go

What She Don't Know

His Dirty Secret

His Dirty Secret: Kim's Story

His Dirty Secret: Charmaine's Story

Enticed By A Kingpin

Falling For The Wrong One

Torn Between A Thug & A Boss

Follow Mia Black on Instagram for more updates: @authormiablack